The Big Island Race

WATCH ON prime video PBS KIDS

W9-AKC-678

Clifford created by
Norman Bridwell

Scholastic Inc.

Written by Meredith Rusu
Illustrated by Jen Oxley

ISBN 978-1-338-54194-6

10 9 8 7 6 5 4 3 2 1   20 21 22 23 24

Printed in Jefferson City, MO, U.S.A. 40 • First edition 2020 • Book design by Betsy Peterschmidt

Scholastic Inc., 557 Broadway, New York, NY 10012
Scholastic UK Ltd., Euston House, 24 Eversholt Street, London NW1 1DB

It was storytime on Birdwell Island. Mrs. Clayton, the librarian, was reading to Emily Elizabeth, Clifford, and their friend Samantha.

The story was about astronauts on a mission to the red planet, Mars.

"I wish we could go into space," Samantha said.

"Let's go on a mission to Mars!" Emily Elizabeth exclaimed.

Just then, the girls' friends Jack and Pablo skated past.

"We loved your space book, Mrs. Clayton!" Pablo called.

"We are going to be the first astronauts on Mars!" Emily Elizabeth told them.

"Not if *we* get there first." Jack grinned.

"It's a space race!" Emily Elizabeth declared.

"The first team to bring back a red stone from Mars wins."

Jack hopped on his skateboard.

Pablo gripped the handles of his scooter.

Emily Elizabeth and Samantha climbed onto Clifford's back.

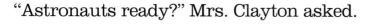

"Astronauts ready?" Mrs. Clayton asked.

"Five . . . four . . . three . . . two . . . one . . . blast off!"

Whoosh! The friends were off, and the space race was on!

Clifford was quick, but Pablo and Jack whizzed past him down the hill.

"They're getting ahead!" cried Samantha.

"Don't worry," said Emily Elizabeth. "We have a big red rocket! Clifford, it's time to blast off!"

But just then, Clifford spotted a man with a tasty-looking sandwich.

His tummy rumbled.

"Clifford, there's no time for a treat right now!" Emily Elizabeth yelped as Clifford veered toward the sandwich.

Clifford knew Emily Elizabeth was right—a real astronaut wouldn't stop for a snack in the middle of a mission.

With a burst of speed, Clifford caught up to Jack and Pablo.

Now the friends were nose and nose! Neck and neck! Scooter and tail!

Fweeeeet!

Ms. Ellerby, the Birdwell Island crossing guard, blew her whistle.

"No scooting or skating in the crosswalk," Ms. Ellerby warned the boys. "And no running on the sidewalk, Clifford."

"Yes, Ms. Ellerby," the children said reluctantly.

The friends started on their way again.

But with Ms. Ellerby watching them, their race was *suuuuper* slow.

That was, until they reached the park.

Then it was GO time!

Clifford's doggy pals Baily and Tucker were playing in the park.

"Hey, Clifford! Do you want to come play with us?" they called.

"I can't play now!" Clifford yelped. "I'm on a mission to Mars!"

"I don't see Jack and Pablo," Samantha realized. "We must be winning!"

Clifford panted. He was getting thirsty.

"Clifford needs to refuel," Emily Elizabeth told Samantha. "Let's make a quick space-station stop at my parents' shop!"

At the Sea Shell souvenir store, Clifford lapped up water from a dog bowl while Emily Elizabeth and Samantha borrowed some binoculars.

"Hi, honey!" Emily Elizabeth's parents waved at the girls.

"No time to talk!" Emily Elizabeth explained. "We're racing Jack and Pablo to Mars!"

"Well, you'd better hurry." Emily Elizabeth's dad pointed. "Jack and Pablo are sailing away on their spaceship."

"We have to beat them!" Emily Elizabeth exclaimed. "Come on—
I know a shortcut."

"Be back on earth in time for dinner!" her dad called.

Emily Elizabeth led Clifford up a steep, rocky hill.

It was hard for the big red dog to balance with so many slipping, sliding rocks.

"This galaxy sure looks a lot like Rocky Point," Samantha said.

Soon, the friends had made it over the rocky terrain and slid safely down to the sand dunes on the other side.

Had their shortcut worked?

Emily Elizabeth looked out over the bay through her binoculars.

There! The red shores of Mars were in sight!

But so were Jack and Pablo!

"They're almost at the red rocks on the beach!" Emily Elizabeth cried.
"They're going to reach Mars before we do!"

"Grrrrwoooof!"

"Not if I can help it!" Clifford told Emily Elizabeth.

The big red dog rocketed across the sand dunes.

His big paws sent sand flying everywhere!

"Go, Clifford, go!" Emily Elizabeth and Samantha cheered.

Jack and Pablo tied up their boat just as Clifford reached the last sand dune.

"They're going to make a run for it!" Emily Elizabeth shouted. "But we can win if we run *really* fast! Go, Clifford!"

Clifford took a flying leap off the sand dune.

But when he landed, his legs sunk straight into the sticky, Martian mud!

Emily Elizabeth tried to push Clifford out, but it was no use.

He was trapped.

"Come on, Emily Elizabeth," Samantha said. "We have to run!"

Emily Elizabeth wanted to win, but not without her best friend.

"It's not worth winning if I have to leave Clifford behind," she said.

Suddenly, Jack and Pablo ran up.

"I guess you two win," Emily Elizabeth said.
"Clifford's stuck."

"Racing is no fun if there's no one to race against," Pablo said.
"We'll help you instead!"

Together, the friends pushed and pulled,
tugged and towed.

It wasn't long before Clifford the
Big Red Rocket was out of the mud and
back into orbit!

As the sun set, the brave explorers headed home.

"Welcome back, astronauts!" Mrs. Clayton greeted them.

The friends proudly produced their Martian treasure.

"A red rock straight from the surface of Mars," they said.

"This is out of this world!" Mrs. Clayton said, impressed. "But which team won the race?"

Emily smiled at her friends.

"When you all work together," she said, "everybody wins!"